LUKE'S

By Elizabeth Winthrop

Illustrated by Pat Grant Porter

PUFFIN BOOKS

For Molly, Charles, and Sara—
all for one and one for all.

E.W.

PUFFIN BOOKS
Published by the Penguin Group
Penguin Books USA Inc., 375 Hudson Street, New York, New York 10014, U.S.A.
Penguin Books Ltd, 27 Wrights Lane, London W8 5TZ, England
Penguin Books Australia Ltd, Ringwood, Victoria, Australia
Penguin Books Canada Ltd, 10 Alcorn Avenue, Toronto, Ontario, Canada M4V 3B2
Penguin Books (N.Z.) Ltd, 182–190 Wairau Road, Auckland 10, New Zealand

Penguin Books Ltd, Registered Offices: Harmondsworth, Middlesex, England

First published in the United States of America by Viking Penguin,
a division of Penguin Books USA Inc., 1990
Published in Puffin Books, 1992

1 3 5 7 9 10 8 6 4 2

LIBRARY OF CONGRESS CATALOGING-IN-PUBLICATION DATA
Winthrop, Elizabeth.
    Luke's bully / by Elizabeth Winthrop; illustrated by Pat Grant Porter.   p.   cm.
    Summary: Skinny, shy third-grader Luke cannot hide from Arthur,
his personal bully, until it is time to pick roles for the class play.
    ISBN 0-14-034329-6
    [1. Bullies—Fiction.   2. Schools—Fiction.]   I. Porter, Pat
Grant, ill.   II.   Title.
PZ7.W768Lu 1992   [Fic]—dc20   92-8157

Printed in the United States of America
Set in Plantin

Contents

Arthur
and the Cupcake

Jane and Luke had lived next door to each other forever. Jane had bright blue eyes and bright red curly hair. People on the street turned around and stared when she walked by. Luke was as skinny as a twig. He had long blond hair that fell in his face. Luke liked to hide behind his hair.

Every day they walked home together from South School. This year they had been put in different sections. Luke missed having Jane in his class because now he was stuck with Arthur Hare. Arthur was the fattest, meanest kid in the third grade. Their desks were right next to each other. Arthur was always staring at Luke's papers and pulling the reading book away from him. They were supposed to share it. Arthur didn't know anything about sharing.

On Monday afternoon, Jane was not waiting in her usual place in front of school. Luke went looking for her. He found her in her classroom emptying wastepaper baskets. She was picking them up and banging them down.

"I can't walk home with you today," she grumbled. "I passed Mary Ann a note about the class play. Mrs. Wilkie caught me."

"I can't wait for you because my mother is taking me to the dentist."

"All right. I'll see you tomorrow then," Jane said. "If I ever get home. After this, I have to wash down the blackboard and straighten the desks. Mrs. Wilkie is mean."

Jane was always in trouble. She couldn't sit

still. She laughed too loud and talked too much and ran too fast in recess. Luke's mother said Jane reminded her of the tornados they used to have back in Oklahoma. Jane's mother agreed.

Luke walked home slowly, dragging his sneakers through the piles of wet leaves. He didn't want to go home. He hated the dentist. He wanted to hide in his secret place under the front hall stairs and read his animal book.

He heard footsteps behind him. Arthur was following him.

Luke began to run. Arthur began to run too.

Arthur caught up with him at the corner of Luke's block.

"Hold it," Arthur said. He grabbed Luke's arm.

"I have to go home," Luke said. "My mother's waiting for me."

"Where's the cupcake?" Arthur snatched Luke's lunchbox. He turned it upside down. A napkin and an empty cupcake paper fell out on to the sidewalk.

"I ate it," said Luke. "It was my cupcake."

"You said you'd give it to me," said Arthur.

"I forgot," said Luke. It wasn't true. He knew he'd promised to give his cupcake to Arthur. But Arthur hadn't come to lunch. He'd been sent to the principal's office. But Luke's cupcake came to lunch. There it was staring up at him with its thick chocolate icing. Maybe Arthur will forget, Luke had told himself when he took the first gooey bite. But Arthur hadn't forgotten.

"You'd better bring me a cupcake tomorrow," Arthur said. "Or you're going to be in big trouble."

Luke walked away as fast as he could. When he looked back, Arthur was still standing on the sidewalk glaring at him. "You'd better not forget," he yelled. Luke pretended not to hear.

"I hate Arthur," Luke said when he got home. He slammed his lunchbox down on the kitchen table.

"*Hate* is a very big word," his mother said. "What's wrong with Arthur?"

"He's a bully," said Luke.

"Well, he's got three older brothers," said his

mother. "It must be tough to be at the end of the line."

Sometimes mothers were no help at all. Luke took a cookie and began to slip out the side door of the kitchen. Maybe his mother had forgotten about the dentist. Maybe the dentist had moved to Australia.

"Don't sneak away, Luke," his mother said without turning around. "Your appointment is in fifteen minutes."

"I hate the dentist," Luke whispered to himself.

The Thanksgiving Play

"What are you going to be in the class play?" Jane asked on the way to school the next day.

"I don't know," said Luke. He didn't have time to think about the play. He was worried about Arthur. All he had in his lunchbox were three extra cookies.

"Do you think three oatmeal cookies equal one chocolate cupcake?" he asked Jane.

"Sure," she said. But Luke knew she wasn't listening. She was still thinking about the play.

Last year, she was the head angel in the Christmas pageant. This year they were doing a Thanksgiving play. She probably wanted to be the head turkey.

"I'm going to be the pilgrim leader," said Jane.

"How do you know?" asked Luke.

"Because I already told Mrs. Wilkie. That's what I want to be."

"The pilgrim leader was a man. You know you don't always get what you want," Luke said grumpily.

"What's wrong with you?"

"Arthur told me to bring a chocolate cupcake to school for him and I don't have one," Luke said.

"Arthur, Smarthur," said Jane. "Why don't you just bop him in the nose?"

Sometimes friends were no help either.

"Because he's bigger than I am," Luke said.

"You want me to bop him in the nose for you?"

"I wish you could," Luke said with a sigh.

"But I'm the one he's picking on. I don't think it would help if you bopped him. Thanks anyway."

At school, Arthur grabbed Luke right outside the classroom door.

"Did you bring it?" he growled.

His breath smelled like peanut butter. Maybe it was time for Arthur to go to the dentist, Luke thought.

"No, I brought something better."

"What is it?"

"It's a secret. Until lunchtime. But there are three of them."

"They better be good," said Arthur.

"Good morning, boys," said Mr. Robbins. "What's all this about?"

"Nothing," Arthur said in a loud, fake voice.

Luke just shrugged and looked at his shoes.

"Nothing looks like it might be something," Mr. Robbins said. He took off his glasses and wiped them clean. Then he put them back on.

Nobody said anything. Arthur was glaring at Luke. Luke hid behind his hair.

"Well, if anybody ever needs to come and talk to me about something, I'd be happy to hear it. Right now, it's time for class to start." He marched between them into the classroom. Arthur stuck his tongue out at Mr. Robbins's back.

"Today we are going to start reading a Thanksgiving story," Mr. Robbins said. He walked down the rows passing out a new book. "Mrs. Wilkie has turned this story into a play. We'll be putting it on the week before Thanksgiving. Tomorrow we'll decide who has which part. Luke, you may start the reading. Loud and clear, please."

Luke loved to read. Most of the time he liked reading out loud in school. But today he read in a very low, quiet voice. He knew that Mr. Robbins was thinking about parts for the play. Luke did not like being in plays. Last year, he had been a duck in the Easter play. The feathers on his costume kept tickling his nose and he sneezed right in the middle of his most important line. Everybody in the audience burst out laughing. Then he had forgotten the rest of his speech. After that, he told Jane he was never going to be in another play. He knew if he read this play loud and clear he would probably be stuck with a turkey costume. More feathers.

"Luke, we can barely hear you," said Mr. Robbins. "Do you have a cold today?"

"No," Luke said. He did not look up from the book.

Nobody said anything for a long time. Luke knew Mr. Robbins was staring at him. This was Mr. Robbins's favorite trick. He could look at people without saying anything for the longest time.

Rachel sniffled in the seat behind Luke. Somebody dropped a pencil case. A chair squeaked.

"All right. Arthur, you may continue with the reading," Mr. Robbins finally said.

Arthur pulled the book away from Luke. That was the worst thing about reading time. Luke always had to share the book with Arthur. When

Arthur read he put his nose down close to the book and sounded out every single letter. Sometimes the sentences came out so slowly that Luke forgot where they were in the story. Then he would try to read ahead over Arthur's shoulder. But Arthur's hair or his chin or his hand always got in the way.

"The pump . . . kin . . . went . . . down . . . the . . . road . . . lick . . . et . . . y-split," read Arthur. Then he rubbed his nose and pushed his finger down to the next line. His finger left a dirty smudge on the page.

Luke's foot began to jiggle under the table. He had already peeked ahead to the part where the pumpkin met the turkey. Luke was dying to know what they said to each other. It would probably take Arthur two weeks to get to that part.

Arthur stopped reading.

"Keep going, Arthur," said Mr. Robbins. "You're doing just fine."

"I can't," said Arthur. "Luke is kicking my foot."

"I'm not," said Luke. "I was jiggling my foot and it just touched him."

"Go ahead, Arthur," said Mr. Robbins in a very patient voice.

"The pump . . . kin . . . rolled . . . down . . . the . . . hill."

Luke's hands began to twitch. He stuck them under his bottom. Then he leaned over and tried to look at Mark's book. But Mark wasn't even on the right page. He had propped the book up so it would hide his rubber band ball.

Mark had started his rubber band ball on the first day of school. He said it was going to be the first rubber band ball in *The Guinness Book of World Records*. It was already the size of a tennis ball.

When reading time was over, Mr. Robbins told everybody to get out their math books. Then he asked Luke to come up to his desk.

"Luke, is something wrong?" he asked in a very quiet voice.

"No," Luke whispered. He was sure everybody was listening to them.

"Is there something going on between you and Arthur?"

"No," Luke said. "I don't want to be in the play."

"But the whole class is going to be in the play," said Mr. Robbins. "And you speak so clearly when you read. I know you'd make a terrific actor."

Luke tried one more time. "I'm shy," he said. That's what his mother always said about him when he hid behind his hair.

"Well, we can work on that," Mr. Robbins said.

The bell rang for recess. Everybody slammed their books shut and scrambled over each other for their coats.

"I am not going to be in the play," Luke said in a very small voice. Nobody heard him.

The Lunch Fight

Luke found Jane out on the playground. She was playing king of the castle on the monkey bars.

"Hey, Luke," she yelled. "Come up here with me."

Together they sat on the very top rung.

"We read the Thanksgiving story in class today," Luke said. "It's dumb."

"The ending is funny," Jane said. "I like the

part when the turkey gets up off the table and runs away."

"We didn't get to the end," Luke said. "Arthur reads too slowly."

"Everybody says that Allen is going to be the head pilgrim because he's the tallest one in the class," Jane said. "I told Mrs. Wilkie that I wanted to be it."

"What did she say?"

"The same thing she always says. 'We'll have to see.' I wish she hadn't caught me passing that note to Mary Ann."

"Will you sit next to me at lunch?" Luke asked. "I don't think Arthur's going to like oatmeal cookies. Peanut butter is Arthur's first favorite thing in the whole world and chocolate is his second favorite. I wonder if my mother knows how to make peanut butter cookies."

"If he gives you any trouble, I'll bop him on the head with my lunchbox. It's very heavy today," Jane said with a giggle. "Mom let me bring a soda to school."

"Here he comes now," Luke said.

18 ·

"Arthur, Smarthur, stick your head in peanut butter," Jane yelled.

"Don't do that," Luke said. "You'll just make it worse."

Arthur started swinging his way up the monkey bars. He looked just like a monkey.

Just then the bell rang. Recess was over.

"Jane and Luke, sitting in a tree," Arthur chanted. "K-I-S-I-N-G. First comes love, then comes marriage . . ."

"You're so dumb you can't even spell *kissing* right," Jane said. She scrambled down the other side of the jungle gym.

Arthur started after her but she skipped away just in time.

At lunch, Luke sat in between Jane and Mark. He hunched his shoulders way down, hoping he would disappear. But it didn't work.

In the middle of his chicken sandwich, somebody poked a finger in his back. It was Arthur. "This is a stickup," Arthur said. "Hand over the loot."

Jane had already finished her soda. She was talking to Mary Ann across the table. Luke jabbed her with his elbow but she didn't pay any attention. She just went right on talking.

"Come on, where is it?" Arthur said. He stuck his face right down by Luke's. There was some peanut butter smeared across his bottom lip. Arthur must eat peanut butter every single day, Luke thought.

Luke handed over the three oatmeal cookies. Arthur looked at them and sniffed. He nibbled one corner.

"They're not chocolate," he said.

Luke didn't say anything.

"I hope they don't have raisins in them," Arthur said. A cookie crumb dropped out of his mouth. "I hate raisins."

Luke was sure he had seen his mother put in raisins. He wasn't going to tell Arthur that. He could hear Arthur smacking away behind him.

"A raisin," Arthur roared. "I told you I hate raisins."

Luke closed his eyes. Everybody turned around and looked at Arthur.

"You'd better bring me a chocolate cupcake tomorrow," Arthur said. He dropped the crumbled cookies on top of Luke's sandwich.

"Arthur, go away, you big bully," Jane yelled. "Why don't you get your own mother to make chocolate cupcakes?"

"My mother's too busy," Arthur said. "She's got a very important new job."

Jane had turned away. She was whispering to Mary Ann again.

"What does she do?" Luke asked. His mother worked at home. She was an accountant. That meant she did other people's math problems for them. Sometimes when Luke got home, he had to be very quiet because she had so many problems to do.

"My mother runs a department store in the mall," Arthur said. He was still talking in a very loud voice.

"She does not," said Mark. "She just makes

the announcements on the loudspeaker. That's what your brother told me."

"That's just the same as running the store," Arthur said, and he punched Mark in the arm. Mark swung back and knocked over Luke's apple juice. Arthur ran around the corner of the table. Mark jumped up and began to chase him. The other kids cheered them on.

"Go get him, Mark," Jane yelled. She was standing on the bench next to Luke.

Luke slipped down under the table and tried to wipe the apple juice off his pants. He hated school when it was like this. He wished he were home under the stairs reading his book.

The Deal

The next day, Mr. Robbins asked Luke to read the last part of the Thanksgiving story.

"The pumpkin and the turkey and the cow and the horse and the pig had a big meeting in the barn," Luke read. He barely moved his lips. He made his voice sound very boring. " 'I give milk for the whole village,' said the cow. 'You don't want me to be the Thanksgiving dinner.' 'I cannot be the Thanksgiving dinner,' said the horse. 'I have to pull the wagon to de-de—' "

Luke stopped. He pretended he did not know how to pronounce the word.

"You know that word, Luke," said Mr. Robbins. "Deliver."

" 'Deliver the ice cream to all the houses in town.' "

Everybody began to squirm in their seats. They usually squirmed when Arthur read. Rachel put up her hand. "Can I read now?" she asked.

"Yes, Rachel," said Mr. Robbins. For once, he didn't even look at Luke. "Go ahead. And read it with spirit, please. Imagine that you are on the stage."

" 'Well, I cannot be the Thanksgiving dinner,' said the pig," Rachel read in a high, squeaky voice. Luke pushed the book over to Arthur. He slid down in his seat. He knew Mr. Robbins was disappointed in him but he didn't care. At least he had stopped reading before they got to the turkey's speech.

At recess time, the whole third grade met in the auditorium. Everybody sat in rows in the metal folding chairs while Jane and Mary Ann handed out copies of the play. Then, one by one, they went up to the stage. They read out the speeches Mrs. Wilkie assigned to them.

Luke was given the pilgrim part to read. He read very slowly and very quietly. Mr. Robbins leaned over and whispered something to Mrs. Wilkie. She marked something down on her paper. Jane glared at him when he went back to his seat. She had been given the pig speech to read. She had sounded like a very angry pig. Arthur read the horse speech. He read it very slowly with his head down close to the paper. Luke thought he looked a little bit like a horse eating some oats. When Arthur finished his speech, he marched up and down the stage pulling an imaginary cart. "Thank you, Arthur," Mr. Robbins said with a smile. "That gives us a good idea of your horse qualities."

When everybody finished reading, the two classes had to sit in their seats for a long time. It looked as if Mr. Robbins and Mrs. Wilkie were having an argument. Finally, Jane put up her hand.

"Yes, Jane," Mrs. Wilkie said.

"I want to be the pilgrim leader," she said. "I thought you might want to know."

"Yes, Jane. You've already told me that," said Mrs. Wilkie.

"I want to be the horse," Arthur suddenly shouted from his seat next to Luke. Everybody turned around and stared at him.

Then Mark yelled out that he wanted to be the turkey. Luke smiled. Suddenly, everybody began to jump up and down and wave their hands in the air. Mr. Robbins looked at Mrs. Wilkie. She nodded and shrugged. He stood up and put up two fingers. That was the third grade signal for silence. "You all read very well today. In fact, you read so well that Mrs. Wilkie and I are having a hard time picking the right people for the right parts. So we've decided that you will all draw your parts out of a hat. That's the only fair way." Mrs. Wilkie began to tear up strips of paper and write names on them.

Everybody groaned. Jane groaned the loudest of all. "I never win things like this," she muttered.

"Now, remember we also need some people to work backstage. They will help make the props and pull the curtain. The backstage crew is just as important as the people in the play."

"Do they get to come out and bow at the end?"
Allen asked.

"Yes, of course they do," said Mrs. Wilkie.

Once the strips of paper were all ready, Mr.
Robbins mixed them in a big black hat from the
costume closet. Everybody pushed and shoved
to get to the front of the line. Luke went to the
very back. Mr. Robbins held the hat high so
nobody could see what they were picking.

Luke got the very last piece of paper. He went
back to his seat without looking at it. Arthur
was sitting next to him.

"What does yours say?" Luke asked.

Arthur showed him. The piece of paper said
BACKSTAGE in big block letters. "Dumb
play," he said.

Luke opened his. HORSE, it said. Arthur
leaned over and looked at it. "That's not fair,"
he yelled. He tried to grab the paper but Luke
shoved it in his pocket.

"I'll make a deal with you," Luke whispered.

Arthur looked suspicious. "I always get in trouble when I make deals with my big brothers."

"This will be a good deal," Luke said.

"What's the deal?" Arthur asked.

"I'll switch papers with you. I'll let you be the horse."

"Okay," Arthur said. "It's a deal." He grabbed for Luke's paper but Luke held it out of reach.

"But you won't bug me about cupcakes anymore, okay?" Luke said.

Arthur frowned. "But I don't get desserts in my lunchbox anymore. My mother says she doesn't have time to make them because of her new job."

"Well, maybe I'll give you some if I have extra," Luke said.

Mrs. Wilkie had put up her two fingers for silence.

"Okay, it's a deal," Arthur said. They switched papers.

"Take your seats, everybody," Mrs. Wilkie said. "We'll go down the rows starting with Jane. Tell me your parts so I can write them down."

"Turkey," said Jane. She looked happy. Luke grinned. He'd better remember to warn her about the feathers.

Mary Ann was the pig. Rachel was the pilgrim leader. Mark was the cow.

"Horse," Arthur said in a loud voice when it was his turn.

"Well, isn't that lucky," said Mrs. Wilkie. "Just what you wanted, Arthur."

"Backstage," Luke said.

Mr. Robbins looked at him with a smile. "And I think maybe Luke got just what he wanted, too," he said.

"All right, everybody," said Mrs. Wilkie. "First rehearsal is tomorrow right after lunch. Remember we only have two weeks to practice. Those of you with speaking parts had better start memorizing your lines. Class dismissed."

Arthur
Comes to Visit

Luke and Jane walked home together that afternoon. Jane was already practicing her lines.

"But I can't be the Thanksgiving dinner," she shouted to the falling leaves. "I am just a poor turkey."

"A poor scrawny turkey," Luke corrected her. He was reading ahead in her script.

"Well, I've almost got it," Jane said. "I bet I know all my lines by tomorrow."

"Why are you in such a rush?" Luke asked. "It will take Arthur the whole two weeks to learn his."

"I heard that," said a voice behind them. "Stick 'em up, Luke. What's in your lunchbox?"

"Arthur, all you ever think about is food," Jane said.

"But we had a deal," Luke said.

"No, we didn't. My fingers were crossed behind my back. Go home and tell your mother I want two chocolate cupcakes for lunch tomorrow."

"What is going on here?" Jane said. "I hate being left out of things."

"Well, Arthur picked—"

Luke stopped in the middle of his sentence. He couldn't talk anymore because Arthur's big smelly hand was clamped down over his mouth.

"You'd better not tell, Luke, or you're in big trouble," Arthur said.

"Let go," Luke said. The words sounded like little tiny mumbles.

Jane whopped Arthur on the arm with her lunchbox. "Let him go, Arthur."

"Do you promise not to say anything?" Arthur asked.

Luke nodded. He thought he might faint dead away on the sidewalk if Arthur didn't let him go. Even Arthur's skin smelled like peanut butter. Jane whopped Arthur again.

Arthur let go. "Remember, a deal's a deal," he said. He shoved his face in Luke's.

"Right," Luke said. "If I don't say a word, you won't bug me about cupcakes?"

Arthur looked confused. "Well, all right," he finally said.

"You learned your lines yet, Arthur?" Jane said.

"No, not yet. We got lots of time."

"I've already learned half of mine," Jane said. "See you," she called as she turned onto her street.

"She's a goody-goody," Arthur said.

"She is not," Luke said. " 'Bye. This is my street."

"Which one is your house?" Arthur asked.

"The yellow one with the blue door," Luke said. "See you."

But Arthur kept walking with him. Arthur walked with Luke up his front path. He followed Luke right in the front door of Luke's house.

"Hi, Mom, I'm home," Luke said.

"I'm in the kitchen," his mother called back.

"Goody," Arthur said. "This whole house smells like chocolate."

"Mom, this is Arthur," Luke said. When his mother looked up from the stove, Luke made a funny face at her. His mother didn't seem to notice. She put out her hand to shake Arthur's.

"Hello, Arthur," she said. "I'm so glad Luke invited you over." Luke rolled his eyes. Sometimes mothers could be so dumb.

"What are you cooking?" Arthur asked.

"Chocolate icing for cupcakes."

Luke groaned. They didn't pay any attention to him.

"Do you like chocolate?" asked Luke's mother.

"It's my favorite," Arthur said. "Except for peanut butter."

"Want to help me stir?"

"Sure."

"Wash your hands first."

That was the best idea his mother had come up with yet, Luke thought. Maybe for a while

Arthur's hands would smell like soap instead of peanut butter.

Arthur stirred chocolate and iced cupcakes and licked the bowl. Luke sat around making faces at his mother.

Finally his mother looked up at the clock. "You'd better be getting home, Arthur," she said.

He squinted up at the kitchen clock. "Yeah, I guess so. What time is it?"

"It's almost six o'clock. Why don't I call your mother? She's probably worried about you."

"Not yet," Arthur said. "She doesn't get home from work until six-thirty, sometimes seven o'clock."

"That's right," said Luke's mother. "I heard your mother has a new job. Is anybody home after school?"

"Usually it's my brother Henry. He's supposed to take care of me, but on Tuesdays he has soccer practice."

"So it's just Tuesdays that you're alone," said Luke's mother.

"I don't like it," Arthur said. "I hate my mother's new job. Now she doesn't even have time to make me peanut butter cookies anymore."

Luke stared at Arthur. He hoped his mother didn't get a job in a department store. He liked having her there when he got home from school.

"Well, why don't you come home with Luke on Tuesday afternoons from now on," Luke's mother asked.

"Mom!" Luke cried.

"It's no fun being with Henry either," Arthur said. "He picks all the TV shows and hides my favorite cereal so I can't have any for snacks."

Oh, great, Luke thought. Now his mother would probably ask Arthur to move in with them.

"Then my brother Randy comes home and they won't let me play baseball with them in the backyard. They say I'm too little to play."

"Well, if it's okay with your mother, you could come here on Tuesdays," Luke's mother said.

"Everybody needs one day off from brothers."

"Sure," Arthur said. "That would be great."

Luke groaned. He decided that some mothers should be shipped out to Australia on the same boat with the dentists.

Luke's mother wrapped up two cupcakes and gave them to Arthur.

"Goody," said Arthur. "One for dinner and one for lunch tomorrow."

After Arthur had left, Luke's mother asked, "Isn't he the boy you said you hated?"

Luke nodded.

"I feel sorry for him," she said. "Big brothers are a pain in the neck. I should know. I had three of them."

"I don't care," Luke said. "You should have asked me before you invited him over."

"I guess you're right, Luke. I'm sorry," his mother said. "But it's just one afternoon a week. That won't be so bad."

"You don't know Arthur," Luke said as he stomped out of the room.

Rehearsal

They rehearsed the play every single day. In the beginning, everybody kept running to the wrong place on the stage and bumping into each other. Some of the kids shouted their lines. Others whispered them. Rachel squeaked them.

"I am looking for a very big fat turkey for the Thanksgiving table," squeaked Rachel.

"She's supposed to be the pilgrim leader and she's using her old pig voice," Luke whispered to Allen. He was working backstage, too.

"I told Mrs. Wilkie I should have been the pilgrim leader," Allen said. "Whoever heard of a girl pilgrim leader?"

Jane has, Luke thought, but he didn't say it out loud. The backstage crew was working on a big barn door. Luke hammered another nail into the wood. It went in crooked. Every time Arthur came backstage he gave Luke a punch on the arm. It made Luke so nervous that he was hammering all the nails in crooked.

"Try not to squeak," Mrs. Wilkie called to Rachel from the back row of the auditorium. She sounded very tired. "I can barely hear you back here. And remember. The part about the Thanksgiving table comes later. This is only Act One. The pilgrims haven't even thought up Thanksgiving yet. You must work harder on memorizing your lines so you can recite them without looking at the script."

Jane was the only one who knew her lines by heart. She should, Luke thought. She recited them all the way to school and all the way home again. Even *he* knew them by heart.

Arthur didn't bug Luke about cupcakes any-more, but the next Tuesday afternoon he came over to Luke's house and ate seven chocolate chip cookies all in a row. Then Luke's mother packed up six more for Arthur's lunchbox.

"Arthur seems very hungry today," said Luke's mother after he left.

"Arthur is always hungry," Luke said. But he didn't really mind. He and Arthur had played basketball out by the garage. It was more fun than playing alone.

By the beginning of the second week, Mr. Rob-bins and Mrs. Wilkie began to look very wor-ried. The kids were still mixing up their lines. Arthur didn't know any of his. He read every-thing with his nose buried in the script.

"Look up and speak to the back of the au-dience, Arthur," Mr. Robbins said.

So Arthur lifted his face and his script at the same time. He shouted with his nose still buried in the paper. "Mr. Robbins," Luke called. "I have an idea. Why don't we make cue cards for everybody with their lines written on them? I can stand in that little space in front of the stage and hold them up."

"I think that's a dumb idea," Arthur said. He pulled his cart across the stage in such a rush that the barn door fell over. Mary Ann screamed and jumped out of the way just in time.

Mr. Robbins threw up his hands. "Arthur, you and Jane and Mark pick up the barn door. Prop it up against the side wall. Then I want everybody to sit down while I talk to Mrs. Wilkie."

Everybody took their seats. Mrs. Wilkie and Mr. Robbins talked and talked. The kids squirmed and whispered. Finally, Mr. Robbins put up two fingers for silence.

"Luke, we've decided that your idea is a good one. We only have three more days until the performance. For those of you who can't memorize your lines, you may read from the cue cards. We are going to go back to the classrooms now. Everybody will copy parts of the script on-to big pieces of poster board. Remember to write clearly."

"That was the dumbest idea I've ever heard of," Arthur said to Luke back in the classroom. "Now we've got to do all this extra work."

"Oh, come on, Arthur. Now you don't have to memorize your lines. You can just read them," Luke said. "This will be much easier."

"Who says?" Arthur shouted. He punched Luke in the arm.

Everybody turned around. "Arthur, bring your work up here, please," Mr. Robbins said.

"I'll get you," Arthur whispered. "Right after school."

When the bell rang, Luke met Jane by the door of her classroom. "Hurry up," he said. "Arthur's really mad at me." He rubbed his arm. "He punched me in class. It still hurts."

"You want to hide out at my house?" Jane asked. "I can show you my turkey costume. It's almost finished. Wait till you see it."

"Okay," Luke said. "Arthur will never find me there."

The costume was laid out on the kitchen table. A note from Jane's mother was pinned to the top.

I've gone down to the store to buy more tail feathers. Back soon. Love, Mom.

"I have to call my mother and tell her where I am," Luke said.

"You can use the phone in the hall while I change," Jane said. "Don't come back in until I'm ready."

After Luke called his mother, he pounded on the kitchen door. "Not yet," said Jane. "I'm not ready."

Finally she threw open the swinging door. "TA-DA!" she cried.

Jane looked great. She had on a pair of yellow tights with orange and brown feathers glued all over them. There were two fat yellow rubber gloves on her feet and two more hanging on either side of her face. Another one flopped over on the back of her head.

I've gone to the
store to buy
more tail
feathers.
Back soon
Love Mom
xxx

"No head feathers," said Luke. "Good work."

"The rubber gloves were my father's idea," Jane said. "He said he never heard of anybody sneezing from rubber gloves. Once we make the tail, we'll be all done."

Suddenly there came a loud knocking at the back door.

"Arthur," said Jane. She opened the broom closet and shoved Luke in. He stood in the dark with his face pressed up against a dust mop. It smelled almost as bad as Arthur's peanut butter skin.

"Who is it?" Jane called.

There was a muffled reply. Then Luke heard, "It's just Mom, Luke. She forgot her keys. You can come out now."

Luke fumbled in the dark, searching for the door handle. At last he found it and stumbled out, blinking in the light.

"Well, look who's here," said Mrs. Kerry. "How long have you been living in our broom closet, Luke?"

"Only ten minutes, Mom. He's hiding from

Arthur," Jane said. She was pulling long lines of tail feathers out of her mother's bag.

"Well, it's an excellent hiding place, Luke," Mrs. Kerry went on. "I've often used it to avoid the vacuum cleaner salesman. Shall I serve your hot chocolate in there? Or would you like it out here on the kitchen table?"

"The table, please," Luke said. He liked Mrs. Kerry. She was always making jokes. And nothing Jane did ever surprised her.

"Have a seat, children. It's turkey-tail time."

They sat in a circle and glued feathers until six-thirty. Then Jane and Mrs. Kerry walked Luke home in case Arthur was lurking in the bushes waiting for him.

Luke's Big Discovery

"I learned my lines," Arthur said to Luke the next day before class. "I don't need to read those stupid cue cards."

Luke was amazed. "How did you do it?" he asked.

"I practiced with my mother. She had to memorize the sales announcements for next week. I helped her with her lines and she helped me with mine." Arthur frowned. "I hope I don't get mixed up."

Luke grinned. "That's right. You don't want the horse to yell, 'Shoppers, on the fifth floor . . .' "

Arthur giggled and covered his ears. "Stop it," he said. "You'll get me all mixed up."

At rehearsal, Arthur pulled his cart across the stage and shouted, "I cannot be the Thanksgiving dinner. I have to pull the wagon to deliver the ice cream to all the houses in town. I am too important. I am strong and hardworking."

Then he stopped.

"Good work, Arthur," Mr. Robbins said. "Go on."

Luke was standing in front of the stage with Arthur's cue card. Mr. Robbins said everybody should have them just in case. Luke held it up. Arthur moved closer. He glared at the cue card. He squinted at it. "And everybody knows how tough my meat is," Luke said in a loud whisper.

"And everybody knows how tough my meat is," Arthur shouted. He stepped even closer to Luke.

"Nobody wants an old tough horse for Thanksgiving dinner," Luke said.

"Nobody wants an old tough horse for Thanksgiving dinner," Arthur shouted. Then he pulled his cart the rest of the way across the stage.

Luke sat back and stared at Arthur. He forgot to turn the cue cards.

"Luke, change the card," Mary Ann said. "You're still holding up Arthur's line."

"Mr. Robbins, can I speak to you, please?" Luke said.

"Can't it wait? We're right in the middle of the scene."

"No," said Luke. "Can I please speak to you right now? In private."

Mr. Robbins looked impatient. "All right, Luke, come backstage with me. Allen, you hold the cue cards for Mary Ann."

"Mr. Robbins, I just figured something out," Luke said. "Arthur can't see the cue cards. That's why he thought they were such a dumb idea."

Mr. Robbins straightened up and looked out across the stage. "He can't see?" he said.

"That's why he always grabs the book from me in class and sticks his nose right down close to it," Luke said.

"It does make sense," said Mr. Robbins. "He's been reading with his script right in front of his face." He took off his own glasses and wiped them clean with his handkerchief. "I think I'll try a little experiment back here. Pick one of Mark's cue cards."

Luke shuffled through his pack.

"Arthur," Mr. Robbins called. "Can you come here a minute?"

Jane was on the stage. She turned around and glared at Mr. Robbins. She didn't like it when people interrupted her.

"Start over again, Jane," said Mrs. Wilkie from the front row. "Take it from the top."

Arthur put down the shafts of his cart. He looked at Luke suspiciously. "I didn't do anything wrong," he said to Mr. Robbins.

"I know that, Arthur. I just want to try a little

experiment back here. Nobody else can see us. Now, Luke's going to hold up a cue card. I want you to stand right in front of me and read it from here."

Luke took six giant steps away from Mr. Robbins and Arthur. He held up the cue card.

"I don't need the cue cards," Arthur said. "I learned all my lines."

"And you did a very good job of it," Mr. Robbins said. "But we're just checking something. All right, Luke, go ahead."

Luke held up one of Mark's cards. Arthur cocked his head first one way and then the other. He tried to move closer but Mr. Robbins held him by the shoulders.

"I can't," he said.

Then Mr. Robbins put his own glasses on Arthur's nose. "Try it now," he said.

" 'I give milk for the whole village,' " Arthur read in his slow bumpy reading voice. " 'You don't want me to be the Thanksgiving dinner.' "

Luke pulled out another card.

" 'What are we going to do?' " Arthur read.

"That's Rachel's line." He giggled. " 'What are we going to do?' " he read again in a high squeaky voice. He looked excited. He pushed Mr. Robbins's glasses up his nose. "Give me another one," he said to Luke.

Luke flipped up another card.

" 'I'm not going to be the Thanksgiving dinner. My pink skin is too pretty.' That's Mary Ann's line."

"Arthur, if you had glasses, you could see this clearly all the time," Mr. Robbins said.

"My father wears glasses," Arthur said. "He's always losing them around the house."

"I'm going to call your mother at work this afternoon. I bet you could have your own pair

of glasses by the day after tomorrow for the dress rehearsal."

"All the kids will laugh at me," Arthur said. "Whoever heard of a horse with glasses?"

"You can hook a pair of blinders on the sides of your glasses," said Luke. "All the old workhorses wore blinders. I saw pictures of them in my animal book."

"That's a good idea, Luke," said Mr. Robbins. "With blinders, Arthur would look even more like a real workhorse."

Arthur wasn't listening. He was moving the glasses up and down in front of his eyes.

"This is fun," he said. "I can even read that exit sign."

"Arthur's getting glasses," Luke said to his mother when he got home that afternoon. She was sitting at her working desk with a pile of math problems stacked up in front of her. "And I'm the one who figured out he needed them."

"How did you do that?" his mother asked. So Luke told her about the cue cards and the reading book in class and Mr. Robbins's experiment. "And he wore Mr. Robbins's glasses the rest of the day. The kids didn't laugh at him. They thought it looked like fun. They all wanted to wear Mr. Robbins's glasses but he wouldn't let them. He said only Arthur was allowed to do it."

"Good for you to figure that out," said Luke's mother. "I do remember now that Arthur kept asking me what time it was last Tuesday. I showed him where the clock was but he still kept asking. I just thought he hadn't learned to tell time yet."

"Where's my animal book? I need to take it in to school tomorrow so I can figure out how to make blinders."

"The usual place. Under the stairs," his mother said as she turned back to her work. "I found a recipe for peanut butter cookies. You can take some to Arthur in your lunchbox, if you want."

"All *right*," Luke said. "Arthur loves peanut butter."

The Play

The morning of the dress rehearsal, Arthur came in with his new glasses. They were round and had red frames. The glass inside them was very thick. Everybody wanted to try them on but Arthur said they couldn't.

"My mother says that nobody should wear them but me," Arthur said in a big important voice. "If you don't need glasses, you can get a headache from wearing them."

"That's right," Mr. Robbins said. "Glasses

are not a toy. Arthur will have to take good care of his. If they break or get lost, they are very expensive to replace."

That afternoon at the dress rehearsal, Mr. Robbins helped Arthur into his horse costume. Then Arthur put his glasses on, and Luke hooked the blinders on either side of them. It looked great.

Now there was only one problem. Arthur was so proud of his new glasses that he read every single one of his lines in his slow reading voice. The horse began to sound very dull. The kids squirmed in their seats the same way they did when Arthur read in class.

In the middle of Arthur's last speech, Mr. Robbins put up his hand. "Hold everything. Luke, put away Arthur's cue cards. Now Arthur, remember that you are a horse. You are not a boy showing off his beautiful new glasses. Try reciting your lines the way you did before you got your glasses."

"But I don't remember them," Arthur cried.

"Just try it," said Mr. Robbins. "Think about

what the horse is trying to do. You are a proud, hardworking horse who pulls the ice cream cart all over town. The town can't do without you. You can't possibly be the Thanksgiving dinner. You're much too important."

Arthur smiled. "Okay, Mr. Robbins. I'll take it from the top," he said.

The play went off almost perfectly. Rachel began to squeak when she saw all those faces staring back at her from the audience, but by the second act she had remembered her pilgrim leader voice. Arthur remembered every one of his lines. He even added a few, but the audience couldn't tell.

Jane remembered all her lines, too. At the end, she scrambled off the Thanksgiving table in such a hurry that one of her floppy yellow feet knocked a pumpkin into Rachel's lap. At the end, the backstage crew joined the rest of the cast and took a bow. Luke tried to bow from his special place down in front where nobody could really see him but Mr. Robbins made him come up on the stage with the others. Then while everybody sang a Thanksgiving song, Arthur pushed Luke into the cart and took him for a ride around the barn door.